Usborne English Rea

Level 3

Dracula

Retold by Mairi Mackinnon
Illustrated by Matteo Pincelli

English language consultant: Peter Viney

Contents

You can listen to the story online here:
www.usborneenglishreaders.com/
dracula

"I hope you've enjoyed your visit, sir." The hotel manager shook Jonathan Harker's hand. "Count Dracula has sent his own coach to drive you to the castle."

His wife looked up from her work. "Castle Dracula? Young man, don't go to that terrible place!"

"Be quiet, woman!" said her husband, but the old lady was holding Jonathan's arm. "If you must go, take this." She put something into his hand. It was a small silver cross. "It will protect you, perhaps. Wear it around your neck."

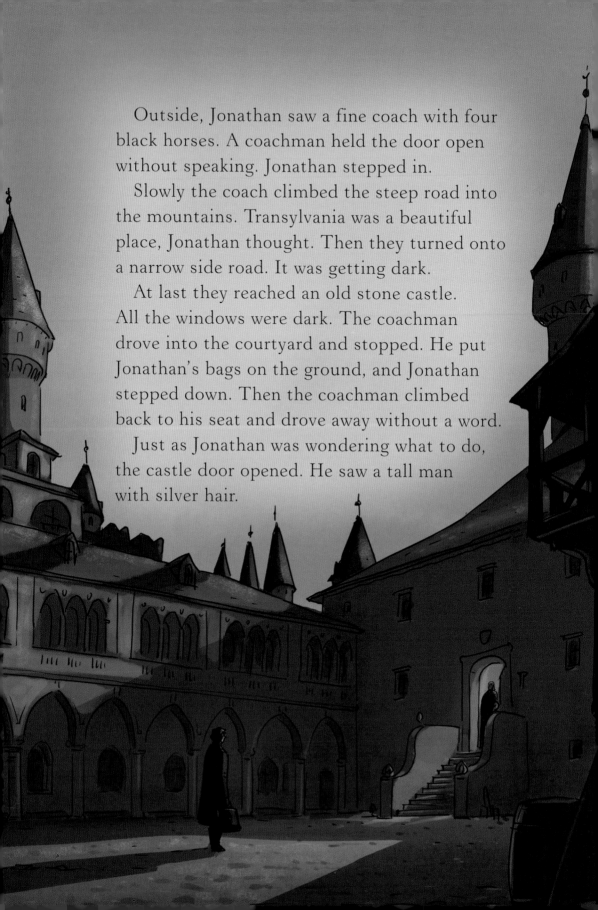

Outside, Jonathan saw a fine coach with four black horses. A coachman held the door open without speaking. Jonathan stepped in.

Slowly the coach climbed the steep road into the mountains. Transylvania was a beautiful place, Jonathan thought. Then they turned onto a narrow side road. It was getting dark.

At last they reached an old stone castle. All the windows were dark. The coachman drove into the courtyard and stopped. He put Jonathan's bags on the ground, and Jonathan stepped down. Then the coachman climbed back to his seat and drove away without a word.

Just as Jonathan was wondering what to do, the castle door opened. He saw a tall man with silver hair.

"Mr. Harker?" he said. "I am Count Dracula." He shook Jonathan's hand. The Count's hand was very cold, Jonathan noticed, and surprisingly strong. Then he picked up Jonathan's bags and led the way to a bedroom in a tower. "When you are ready, you will find some dinner next door. I have already eaten, but I would like to sit with you."

The dinner was excellent. Jonathan was surprised not to see any servants, but he had a pleasant conversation with the Count. "Tell me about the house you have found for me," the old man said.

"It's called Carfax, and it's just outside London," said Jonathan. "It's very private. Nobody has lived there for years."

"It sounds perfect," said the Count.

Jonathan woke late the next morning. He dressed and started shaving.

"Good morning," said the Count. Jonathan turned around quickly. He hadn't seen anything in his small travel mirror.

"You've cut yourself," said the Count. His voice sounded strange. He stepped closer, then saw the silver cross and stopped. Suddenly he reached for the mirror. "Why did you bring this ugly thing?" He opened a window and threw it out, then quickly left the room.

Jonathan looked out of the window. The castle wall was built on steep rock. He couldn't see any other buildings nearby.

He found some breakfast in the room next door, and a message:

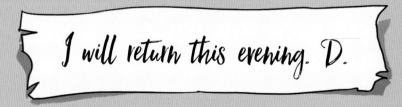

I will return this evening. D.

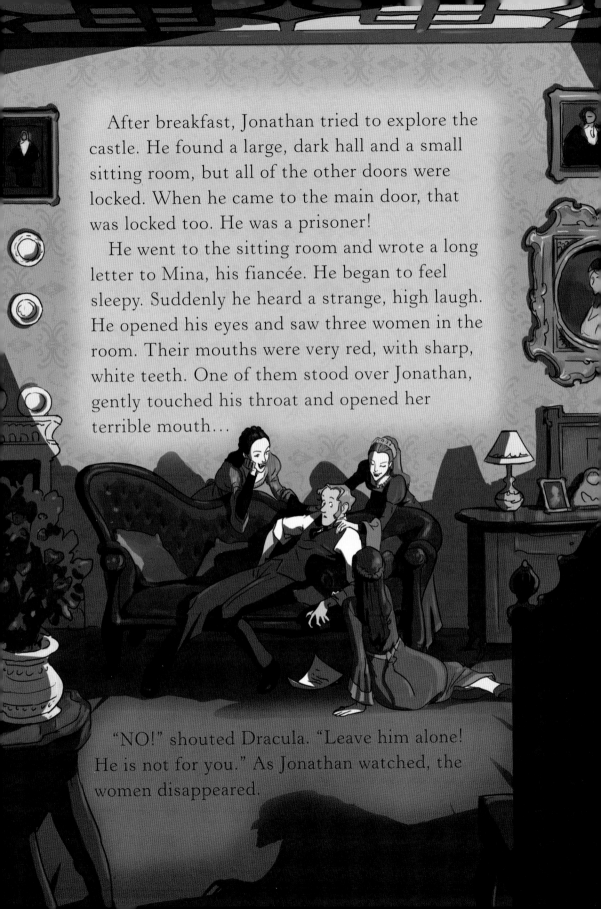

After breakfast, Jonathan tried to explore the castle. He found a large, dark hall and a small sitting room, but all of the other doors were locked. When he came to the main door, that was locked too. He was a prisoner!

He went to the sitting room and wrote a long letter to Mina, his fiancée. He began to feel sleepy. Suddenly he heard a strange, high laugh. He opened his eyes and saw three women in the room. Their mouths were very red, with sharp, white teeth. One of them stood over Jonathan, gently touched his throat and opened her terrible mouth…

"NO!" shouted Dracula. "Leave him alone! He is not for you." As Jonathan watched, the women disappeared.

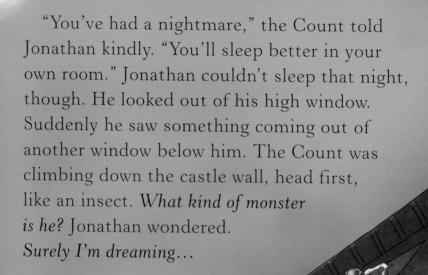

"You've had a nightmare," the Count told Jonathan kindly. "You'll sleep better in your own room." Jonathan couldn't sleep that night, though. He looked out of his high window. Suddenly he saw something coming out of another window below him. The Count was climbing down the castle wall, head first, like an insect. *What kind of monster is he?* Jonathan wondered. *Surely I'm dreaming…*

He woke
in daylight.
He heard noises
from the courtyard,
and hurried to a window.
Some men were lifting large,
heavy boxes into a cart.
Jonathan shouted and waved,
but they just looked up and laughed.
Then they drove away.

Jonathan went back to his bedroom. Could he climb the walls, too? It was a frightening idea – but staying in the castle was even more frightening. He climbed down carefully to the window below, then stepped inside.

He was in a dark, dusty old chapel. A few more boxes were in the middle of the floor. Jonathan opened one: it was full of earth. He opened another, and almost screamed. The Count was lying with his eyes open. He didn't seem to see Jonathan. There was blood around his mouth.

Jonathan ran through the castle. Somehow, he had to find a way out.

"Mina!" Mina looked around the busy station at Whitby and saw her friend Lucy. "Mina, I'm so glad to see you. We're going to have a wonderful holiday."

"Thank you for inviting me – but Lucy, tell me about your news. Two men asked to marry you in one day!"

"They did! I felt sorry for poor Dr. Seward. He's such a nice man – but dear Arthur had asked already. And how is your Jonathan? I'm sorry, is something wrong?"

"I haven't heard from Jonathan since he left for Transylvania," Mina said. "I'm worried about him."

"Oh, Mina, it'll be all right. Letters can easily get lost. He'll soon be home."

That afternoon, the girls walked around the town. Lucy talked happily about her fiancé and their plans for the wedding. Mina noticed dark clouds above the sea. "I think a storm is coming. I hope all the ships are safe."

The next morning, Lucy's mother told them an extraordinary story. "A ship sailed into the port last night, in the storm. It didn't stop until it crashed into the stone wall. Then a huge black dog jumped off it and ran away. When the police arrived, they found the captain, tied to the ship's wheel – dead. There was nobody else. The only cargo was fifty boxes of earth."

"Weren't there any other sailors?" Mina asked.

"They found a diary in the captain's pocket. The ship came from Varna, in Bulgaria. When they started, there were eight more sailors, but they disappeared one by one. They said they had seen a strange, tall man – they were sure that there was something evil on that ship!"

Mina didn't sleep very well. In the middle of the night, she realized that Lucy's bed was empty. She looked out and saw Lucy in her nightdress, walking up the hill.

Mina dressed quickly and followed her friend. She soon saw Lucy sitting near the old ruined church. At first, Mina thought there was someone beside her, but when she arrived, Lucy was alone and asleep.

"Lucy? Are you all right?"

"Mina! How did I get here? Was I sleepwalking?"

"Probably! Come back to the house now. Oh – have you hurt your neck?"

"I don't think so. I don't feel anything. Let's go back, then."

In the morning Lucy's mother had some news. "Look, Mina, there's a letter for you."

Mina opened it. "It's about Jonathan," she said. "He's in hospital – he's been very ill, but he's getting better now. I must go to him. Lucy, I'm sorry to leave so soon."

"I understand," said Lucy. "Of course you must go."

Mina almost didn't recognize the thin, pale man in the hospital gardens.

He looked up. "Mina! Is it really you?"

"Jonathan, my poor dear! What happened to you?"

"I don't remember much. The nurses say I had terrible nightmares when I first arrived. I talked in my sleep about monsters. I know I wrote everything in my diary at the castle, but I daren't read it. Dear Mina, take it. One day you may need to understand."

Arthur was visiting Lucy at her home, in London. He had brought his friend, Dr. Jack Seward. He didn't know that Jack had also asked to marry Lucy.

"I hope you don't mind, my dear," Arthur said, "but I'm worried about you. You look more pale and tired every day."

Jack looked at her closely. "Have you had an accident?"

"No, why?"

"I think you have lost some blood."

"That's not possible," said Lucy's mother. "We haven't left the house since we came back from Whitby."

"Maybe you should have a blood transfusion," said Jack. "I'd like to ask my old professor for advice. He is a wonderful doctor and an extraordinary man. He should reach London tomorrow from Amsterdam."

The next evening, he introduced Professor
van Helsing. The professor was shocked when
he saw Lucy. She was lying in bed and extremely
pale. "You were right to call me. She must have
the transfusion immediately. I have everything
we need – except the blood."

"Please, let me give her mine, sir," said Arthur.
When van Helsing pushed back the
bedclothes, he noticed two marks on Lucy's
neck. "This… this is very bad. I only hope we
are not too late."

After the transfusion, Lucy looked much
better. She opened her eyes. "Thank you,
Arthur, my love," she said.

"Someone must stay beside her," said the professor. "Don't open the windows. I will send some flowers, and you must put them around her bed. We can still save her, my friends." He left with Dr. Seward.

"Save her from what?" asked Lucy's mother. "Don't worry, Arthur, you can go. I'll sit with her."

A little later, the flowers arrived. Lucy's mother looked at them. "No, this must be a mistake. Smelly garlic flowers? Take them to the kitchen." She went back to Lucy's room. "It's too warm in here," she said. "Surely Lucy needs air." She opened a window, and fell backwards. A huge wolf jumped into the room. Lucy screamed.

Arthur, Jack and the Professor arrived at the house the next morning, but nobody opened the door. Finally they forced a window open and climbed in.

They found the servants lying on the floor. "They're deeply asleep," said Jack. "This isn't natural." Upstairs they found Lucy, paler than ever but still alive. Her mother wasn't so lucky.

"Poor, foolish woman," said the Professor.

"She had a weak heart, I know," said Arthur. "Look at her face! Whatever she saw, she was absolutely terrified."

The Professor and Jack couldn't wake Lucy at all. "The marks on her throat – they're bigger," said Jack.

"Yes, I noticed that," said the Professor. "We must find those garlic flowers. She must not be left alone. I will explain everything later."

All day Lucy slept. In the evening, the three men were with her when she suddenly opened her eyes and sat up.

"Arthur, my love! Let me kiss you!" She held out her arms, and Arthur started forward.

"NO!" said the Professor. He held Arthur back. Lucy's eyes were wild and her teeth were long and sharp. She fell back and closed her eyes. When she opened them again, her face was peaceful. "Thank you, Professor," she whispered. "Goodbye, Arthur. Goodbye, dear friends." She was dead.

A few days later, Jack had a visitor.
"Professor! I thought you had gone home."

Van Helsing showed him a newspaper
story. Jack read: "Children disappearing near
graveyard… found hours later, pale but unhurt…
stories of a 'beautiful lady'… what is this?"

"I visited one of these children," said van
Helsing. "The newspaper is almost correct. The
boy was well, but on his neck he had two small
marks."

"Like Lucy's!"

"Exactly. Jack, I want you to come to the
graveyard with me tonight."

A few hours later, they were outside Lucy's
family tomb. "Surely you're not going to open it?"
said Jack; but the Professor unlocked the door.

Jack was even more shocked when his friend began to open Lucy's coffin.

The coffin was empty.

"Someone has taken the body," whispered Jack.

"It's worse than that," said the Professor. "Follow me."

He closed the door, and they walked through the graveyard. Jack saw a white shape, and heard a voice: "Come to me, little one. Let me kiss you." It was Lucy! She seemed to be talking to a small child; but the voice wasn't Lucy's at all.

"Stop!" shouted van Helsing. He held up a cross, and the terrible thing hissed angrily. It flew across the graveyard, and passed through the door of the tomb.

Mina and Jonathan had arrived in London. At their hotel, a letter was waiting.

"Oh, Jonathan, I don't believe it," said Mina. "Lucy and her mother – both dead. How terrible for poor Arthur. I must visit him."

When she arrived, Arthur looked exhausted. "Thank you for coming," he said. "I know how much you loved Lucy." He introduced Jack and the Professor. "We did everything we could," he said.

Van Helsing said to Mina, "So you were with Lucy in Whitby?"

"Yes," said Mina. "My fiancé – my husband, now – had to travel to Transylvania, and Lucy's mother invited me to stay. I wasn't there for very long, in the end." She started crying.

"Transylvania," repeated the Professor quietly. "I am beginning to understand."

After Mina had left, the Professor spoke to Arthur and Jack. "This will be hard for you, Arthur, I know. I have spoken to Mina, and tomorrow I will meet her husband Jonathan. They are good, brave people. Jonathan doesn't know this, but his Count Dracula is something very old, and very evil. People think he is just a story to frighten naughty children; but he is real, and he is here in London. Have you heard of vampires?

Arthur looked pale. "Are you saying that Lucy..?"

"Dracula is trying to make her into a vampire," said the Professor. "Then, unless we can stop her, she will make more vampires. There will be no end."

"What do we have to do?" asked Jack.

The friends arrived at the graveyard in the late afternoon. The Professor opened the tomb, then opened the coffin. Lucy was lying with her eyes open. They could see her sharp teeth.

Arthur held a wooden stake. His hands were shaking.

"Remember, this is not Lucy," said the Professor. "Do this, and the real Lucy will have peace."

Arthur drove the stake into the vampire's heart. The thing screamed horribly, then there was silence. The sharp teeth had gone. Lucy's face was gentle and calm.

"You did well," said the Professor. "And now we must stop Dracula's plans."

Later, Jonathan told them about his visit to the castle.

"We should go to this Carfax House," said the Professor. "Jonathan, will you join us?" Mina wanted to come too, but they persuaded her to stay at the hotel.

They arrived the next morning. A cart was just leaving the house, carrying twelve large boxes.

"Those look heavy!" said Arthur "Where are you taking them?"

The carters mentioned various places in London. "We're coming back for more tomorrow," they added. "The old man is sending them all over the city." They drove away.

"Quickly, find the chapel!" said van Helsing. They found a broken door at the back of the house. Inside, there was dust everywhere. They soon reached the chapel.

The professor counted. "Thirty-seven boxes here. There were fifty, but the carters took twelve. One is missing!" He started opening the boxes. They were full of earth, as Jonathan remembered. "The vampire must sleep on earth from his homeland," the professor explained. "Let's make it difficult for him."

In each box, he placed a small silver cross. "This is the vampire's poison."

Something moved in the corner of the chapel. Soon hundreds of dark shapes covered the floor. "Rats!" said Jack. "I've never seen so many!"

"*He* is sending them," said the professor. "We must go!" Outside the house, he said, "He will know that we were here; but he won't know that we saw the cart. Carts travel slowly – we'll find those boxes!"

Jonathan returned to the hotel. Mina seemed pale. "You look tired, my love."

"I don't know why. I was asleep just now. I think I had a nightmare… What's that noise, outside the window?"

"It looks like a large bat. Why won't it go away? Shoo!" Jonathan opened the window, and a huge black shadow rushed into the room. Mina screamed.

An hour later, the others were outside the door. "Why don't they answer?" said Arthur.

The Professor forced the door open. Jonathan was lying on the floor. Mina seemed to be asleep in a chair, and above her was the Count, with his mouth at her throat.

"Dracula! Leave now!" The Professor lifted his silver cross. The vampire hissed and disappeared through the open window. The Professor touched Mina's head with the cross, and she screamed: "It's burning me!"

Jonathan tried to stand up. "What happened?"

Mina was crying. "He – he drank my blood, and he made me drink his! He has become a part of me – it's horrible!"

"We will stop him," said Arthur. "We'll save you, Mina."

"Close the window, and keep the cross beside you," said the Professor. "Rest while you can. We'll start the chase tomorrow."

The next morning, the Professor asked Mina, "Did you sleep at all?"

"He was in my dreams," she said; "but it made me think. If he is watching us now, perhaps there is a way for us to watch him? Professor, Jack told me that you can hypnotize people."

"Excellent idea!" said the Professor. Mina sat down, and he moved his hands in front of her face until her eyes closed.

"What can you see?" he asked.

She answered in a low voice. "Everything is dark. I can hear water beside me, and footsteps and voices above. We are moving, slowly."

"He's on a ship!" guessed Arthur.

"He is returning to his homeland," said the Professor. "He feels strongest there. Arthur, will you go to the port, and find out whatever you can?"

Arthur was soon back. "A ship left this morning for Varna. Just before it sailed, a tall man paid a lot of money to travel with a big, heavy box."

"The missing box!" said Jack.

"We can reach Varna much faster by land than by sea," said Jonathan. "We'll travel by train, and wait for him. Thanks to Mina, we'll know exactly what he's doing."

A few days later, they arrived in Varna. Every morning, the Professor hypnotized Mina. The answer was always the same: dark, the sound of water, moving slowly. Arthur arranged for messages from ports along the way: if the ship stopped anywhere, he would know.

One morning, when the Professor hypnotized her, Mina said, "The water is quiet. I am being carried upwards."

A moment later, Arthur rushed into the room. "A message – from Galatz. The ship is in the port there. It arrived last night, in thick fog."

"But that's far north of here," said Jack. "Why didn't it come to Varna?"

"Galatz is on the river," said the Professor. "If the Count travels up the river in his box, he can come quite close to his castle. That way, he will save his strength. I believe he is expecting us now."

"Can we follow him?" asked Arthur. "I'll pay for a fast boat."

"The train to Galatz is faster," said the Professor. "Then Mina and I will go by coach, and you others can chase him along the river. He will not escape us."

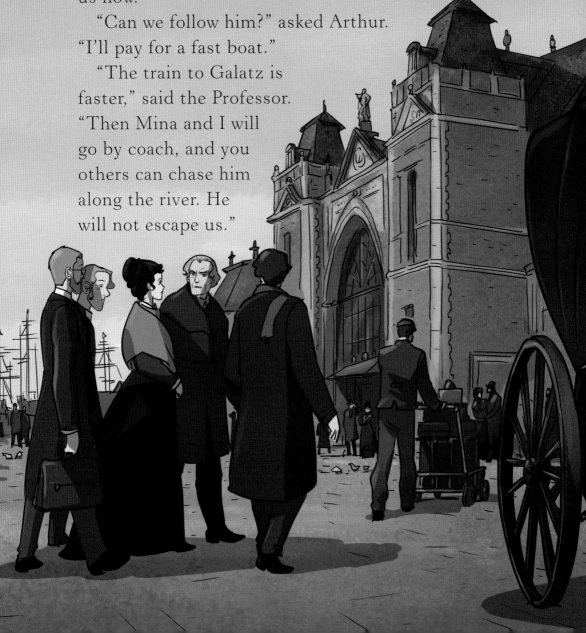

Mina and the Professor went as far as they could by coach, but the weather was getting worse. It had started to snow. "We'll leave the coach and take the horses," the Professor said.

The snow fell faster. "You're tired, and we won't reach the castle tonight," he told Mina. "Let's find somewhere to rest. Look, there's a cave. I'll make a fire, and we'll have something to eat."

Mina wasn't hungry. She desperately wanted to sleep. Suddenly she and the Professor saw three pale women on the other side of the fire. "Come to us, sister," they said. Mina started to move.

"No!" said the Professor. He walked towards the women, holding the silver cross. They hissed and disappeared. The Professor stayed awake for the rest of the night, but the women didn't come back.

In the morning, Mina was deeply asleep. The Professor placed the cross above the cave entrance, wrote a short message and took one of the horses.

The snow had stopped, and he soon saw the castle. The main door wasn't even locked. He remembered Jonathan's story, and found the way to the chapel.

In the walls at the sides
were four stone tombs, one larger
than the others. Carefully, the Professor
opened the three smaller tombs. In each one,
a vampire woman was lying with her eyes open,
unseeing. The professor drove stakes into their
hearts. There were three terrible screams, and
the three bodies immediately turned to dust.

On the largest tomb, the professor read
one word:

DRACULA

The tomb itself was empty.

"So he has not come back," said the
Professor. "I'll make sure he never will."
He left one silver cross in the tomb,
another over the chapel window and a
third above the entrance to the castle.
Finally he rode back to Mina.

Arthur, Jack and Jonathan's boat had sailed quickly at first, but then the river became narrower and full of rocks. Eventually they came to a village.

"There's a boat there!" said Arthur.

"Look on the road above," said Jack. They could see a heavy cart, slowly climbing the hill.

"We'll have to continue on land anyway," said Arthur. "We'll need horses."

"We must hurry," said Jonathan. "Think of Mina!"

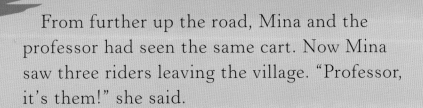

From further up the road, Mina and the professor had seen the same cart. Now Mina saw three riders leaving the village. "Professor, it's them!" she said.

"Look, the cart is going as fast as it can – but they're going to catch it." Mina started running down towards the group, and the Professor followed.

The riders were close to the cart now. "Stop!" shouted Arthur. He and the others took out their guns, but the carters had long, sharp knives. Jonathan and Jack rushed through the men, and Jonathan pushed the heavy box to the ground. It fell open and everyone saw the Count's cruel face.

The terrified carters ran. Jonathan took a sharp stake out of his coat and drove it into the Count's heart. As they watched, the old vampire turned to dust.

"Jonathan!" shouted Mina.

"That's the end of him," said Jonathan.

"It's the end of me, too, I'm afraid," said
Jack. He was lying on the ground, bleeding.
"One of the carters' knives…"

"Oh, can't we do anything?" asked Mina.

Jack lifted his arm towards her. "It was worth
it," he said. "Look!"

"The burn mark, from the Professor's silver
cross," said Arthur. "It's gone!"

Mina was smiling and crying at the same
time. "Jack, how can we thank you?"

"Bravest of men, and best of friends," said
Jonathan. "We will never forget you."

About the story

Abraham 'Bram' Stoker was born in Ireland in 1847. He became interested in acting while he was at university, and wrote about plays for a Dublin newspaper. In 1876, he met the famous English actor, Henry Irving. They became friends, and Irving asked Stoker to come to London and work for him. Stoker lived in London for the rest of his life.

Bram Stoker never visited Transylvania (now part of Romania in Eastern Europe), but he did visit the town of Whitby. While he was there, he began working on a story inspired by the vampire legends of Eastern Europe. This, of course, was *Dracula* (Stoker originally called it *The Un-Dead*). Prince Vlad III of Transylvania (1428-1476), also known as Dracula, was a real person, and gave his name to the vampire.

The book wasn't an immediate success. However, it inspired many film versions, and these persuaded more and more people to read the original. It is now recognized as one of the classic horror stories of all time.

Activities

The answers are on page 48.

A visit to Castle Dracula

Can you put these pictures and sentences
in the right order?

A.

"Tell me about the house
you have found for me"

B.

There was blood around
the Count's mouth.

C.

The Count was
climbing like an insect.

D.

"Leave him alone!
He is not for you."

E.

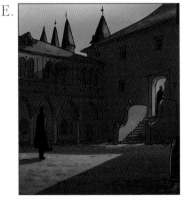

The coachman drove
away without a word.

F.

"Don't go to that
terrible place!"

Who's who

Find *two* sentences which describe each character.

Jonathan

Mina

Lucy

A.
He doesn't appear
in Jonathan's
travel mirror.

B.
He realizes that
he is a prisoner
in the castle.

C.
Two men ask
to marry her
in one day.

D.
She is worried
about her fiancé.

E.
He sends garlic
flowers to Lucy.

F.
She needs
a blood
transfusion.

Professor van Helsing   Arthur   Count Dracula

G.
He asks Jack
to come to the
graveyard at night.

H.
He drives
a stake into
Lucy's heart.

I.
He makes Mina
drink his blood.

J.
She asks the
Professor to
hypnotize her.

K.
He tells his friends
that Dracula's ship
is in Galatz.

L.
He pushes the
heavy box from the
cart to the ground.

Terrible evil

Choose a word from the list to finish each sentence.

1.

They found the ...., tied to the ship's wheel.

2.

She saw Lucy in her ....

3.

"I think you have lost some ...."

4.

Children were disappearing near the ....

5.

"Dracula is trying to make her into a ...."

6.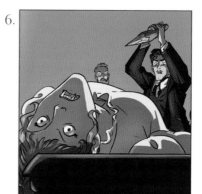

Arthur held a wooden ....

blood

captain

cargo

castle

dream

graveyard

hospital

manager

nightdress

professor

stake

vampire

The chase

Which one is true? Choose a sentence for each picture.

1.

   A. Mina is able to watch Dracula in her dreams.

   B. Mina is able to watch Dracula when she is hypnotized.

2.

   A. Dracula's ship is in the port at Galatz.

   B. Dracula's ship has arrived in Varna.

3.

   A. The Professor finds Dracula in the largest tomb.

   B. The Professor makes sure Dracula can never come back.

4.

   A. The old vampire crumbles to dust.

   B. The old vampire attacks Jack Seward.

Word list

bat (n) a small animal that looks like
a mouse with wings, and flies at night.

bedclothes (n) the sheets and blankets on a bed.

cargo (n) when someone pays for something
to be transported by ship, it's called cargo.

cart (n) something with wheels for moving or carrying
heavy things. Carts are usually pulled by horses.

chapel (n) a room that is like a small church inside
a private house, a castle or another building.

chase (n) a hunt for a person or an animal.

church (n) a building where Christians
come together to worship and pray.

coach (n) something that you ride in, usually pulled by horses.

coffin (n) the wooden box that dead people are buried in.

Count (n) a type of lord who is almost as important as a prince.

courtyard (n) an outdoor space surrounded
by buildings or parts of a building.

cross (n) the Christian symbol †.

diary (n) a book in which you write everything that happens to you,
or everything that you need to do on dates or at times in the future.

drive, drove (v) as well as driving a car or a coach, you can
drive by pushing something hard into something else.

earth (n) you grow plants in earth.
Usually it is a thick, brown powder.

extraordinary (adj) very surprising and unusual.

fiancé, fiancée (n) the person you are going
to marry. Fiancé is male, fiancée is female.

garlic (n) a plant often used to give food a strong taste.

graveyard (n) the area, usually next to
a church, where dead people are buried.

hiss (v) the 'sssss' noise that a snake makes, for example.

hypnotize (v) when you hypnotize someone, they seem to be asleep but they can move, answer you and do what you say.

manager (n) in a hotel, the manager organizes the other workers and makes sure that they take good care of the guests.

port (n) a place where ships bring cargo to land, and where they can be safe from storms and bad weather.

professor (n) a university teacher with special knowledge of a particular subject.

rat (n) an animal like a large mouse. Rats often spread illness, and many people dislike them.

shave (v) a man shaves his chin to remove the hair that would grow into a beard.

sleepwalk (v) when a person walks at night without waking up, they are sleepwalking.

stake (n) a piece of wood, cut to a point at one end.

strength (n) the noun from 'strong'; a kind of power.

throat (n) the front part of your neck. You use your throat to swallow food and drink.

tomb (n) a place where a person is buried, either in a chapel or in a graveyard. Tombs are made of stone, and often look like small buildings.

transfusion (n) when one person's blood is used in another person's body to keep that person alive or help them to get better, it is a blood transfusion.

turn (v) when something turns to something else, it becomes something else; for instance, ice turns to water.

vampire (n) a monster that was once human, and can now live for hundreds of years by drinking other people's blood.

(to be) worth it when something is difficult or expensive but you are glad that you did it, you might say 'it was worth it'.

Answers

A visit to Castle Dracula

F, E, A, D, C, B

Terrible evil

1. captain
2. nightdress
3. blood
4. graveyard
5. vampire
6. stake

Who's who

Jonathan - B, L
Mina - D, J
Lucy - C, F
Professor van Helsing - E, G
Arthur - H, K
Dracula - A, I

The chase

1. B
2. A
3. B
4. A

You can find information about other Usborne English Readers here: usborneenglishreaders.com

Designed by Jodie Smith

Series designer: Laura Nelson Norris

Edited by Jane Chisholm

With thanks to Andy Prentice

Page 40: portrait print of Bram Stoker © Charles Walker / TopFoto.co.uk

First published in 2019 by Usborne Publishing Ltd.,
Usborne House, 83-85 Saffron Hill, London EC1N 8RT, England.
usborne.com Copyright © 2019 Usborne Publishing Ltd.